Series 563

GOING TO
SCHOOL

A LADYBIRD LEARNING TO READ BOOK

Text by
M. E. GAGG, N.F.U.

Illustrated by
J. H. WINGFIELD

Publishers : Wills & Hepworth Ltd., Loughborough

First published 1959   *Printed in England*

We go
into school.

7214 0051 5

We take off
our coats
and hats.

We go into
our classroom.

We tidy
the nature table.

horse
chestnut
leaves

marsh
marigolds

bird's nest

tadpoles

bluebells

clover

violets

We give
the flowers
some water.

We feed
the hamster.

We say
our prayers.

Then we write
our news.

John and I are going to school

We read
in the
book corner.

We measure
and we weigh.

We buy things at the shop.

Then we have
our milk.

We play
in the
playground.

We take off
our frocks
and shirts
and we change
our shoes.

We dance
to the music.

We sing songs.

Then we wash
our hands.

We have
our dinner.

After dinner
we paint.

We make things
with wood.

We make things
with clay.

We tidy
our classroom.

We listen
to a story.

We can tie our
shoe laces

Peter
Susan   John
David   Mary
Judy

Today
it is

Sunny

Then we put on
our coats
and hats
and go home.

Series 563